Published 2016 by Geddes & Grosset,
an imprint of The Gresham Publishing Company Ltd,
Academy Park, Building 4000, Gower Street,
Glasgow, G51 1PR, Scotland.

Illustrations by Sue King.

ISBN 978-1-910965-51-1

Printed and bound in Malaysia.

First Steps

Splash!

by
Judy Hamilton

Standing on the silver sand
Right beside the sea,
Pick up a pebble, toss it in,
One, two, three ...

SPLASH!

Helping after dinner,
  Standing on a chair,
Sink full of water,
  Bubbles everywhere!

Two soapy saucepan lids,
  Bish-bish bash,
Bubbly water dripping off,
  splish-splosh ...

SPLASH!

Fill up the paddling pool
With water to the brim.

It's a sunny day!
The water's warm!
Come on! Jump right in!

SPLASH!

Look at all the rain clouds
Covering the sun!
Dreary drippy weather –
But we're having fun!

Coats on! Boots on!
  Squidge through the mud!
Ooh, look! A puddle! Shall we?
  Do you think we should ...?

SPLASH!

Mr Jones has a great big brolly
To keep his best suit dry.

He's nearly home!
He's almost there!
   Then a great big bus comes by ...

SPLASH!

When Dad helps out at bathtime,
There's water all over the place,
He helps us wash our dirty feet ...

And then we wash his face!

SPLASH!

Out walking by the lake
with our dog Jim,
Dad throws a stick and
Jim jumps in ...

Jim swims out to fetch the stick
Then scrambles from the lake,

And then we all stand back
While he gives himself a shake!

SPLASH!

Time for a nice cool drink –
Fill the cup right up!
Creamy white milk pours in
Till it reaches the top.

Watch out! The cup's full!
It can't hold any more!
Too late! Milk spills
All over the floor!

SPLASH!

Watering the flowers
  On a hot summer's day,
We're doing very nicely ...

Then Dad gets in the way!

SPLASH!

Feeling sleepy, snug in bed,
  Listening to the rain,
Tippy-tappy noises
  As it hits the windowpane.
It's nice to be warm and dry,
  Curled up very tight,

Close the curtains,
  Shut out the rain,
It's time to say goodnight!

(SPLASH!)